Zoë and her Zebra

For my children, Jack, Kate and Tom — C. B.

Barefoot Beginners
an imprint of
Barefoot Books, Inc.
41 Schermerhorn Street, Suite 145
Brooklyn, New York
11201-4845

ISBN 1 902283 75 9

This book is printed on 100% acid-free paper

This book was typeset in Greymantle and Charcoal
The illustrations were prepared in felt with braid, buttons,
beads and assorted bric-a-brac

Graphic design by Amesbury Grzelinski Ltd, England
Color separation by Grafiscan, Italy
Printed and bound in Singapore by Tien Wah Press (Pte) Ltd

1 3 5 7 9 8 6 4 2

Zoë and her Zebra

Clare Beaton

BAREFOOT BOOKS

**is for Alice —
but who is chasing her?**

is for Ben —
but who is chasing him?

**is for Carla —
but who is chasing her?**

Dd is for Dylan —
but who is chasing him?

Ee is for Erin — but who is chasing her?

**is for Farooq —
but who is chasing him?**

Gg

**is for Gopinder —
but who is chasing her?**

is for Hamadi —
but who is chasing him?

**is for India —
but who is chasing her?**

J j is for Jacob —
but who is chasing him?

is for Kylie —
but who is chasing her?

is for Luke —
but who is chasing him?

**is for Martha —
but who is chasing her?**

**is for Naiser —
but who is chasing him?**

is for Olga —
but who is chasing her?

P p is for Pedro —
but who is chasing him?

**is for Queenie —
but who is chasing her?**

is for Reuben —
but who is chasing him?

**is for Sita —
but who is chasing her?**

Tt

is for Takeshi —
but who is chasing him?

is for Ursula —
but who is chasing her?

**is for Victor —
but who is chasing him?**

is for Wendy —
but who is chasing her?

**is for Xavier —
but who is chasing him?**

is for Yoko —
but who is chasing her?

**is for Zoë —
but who is she chasing?**

donkey

elephant

hors

bear

cat

fox

alligator

goat

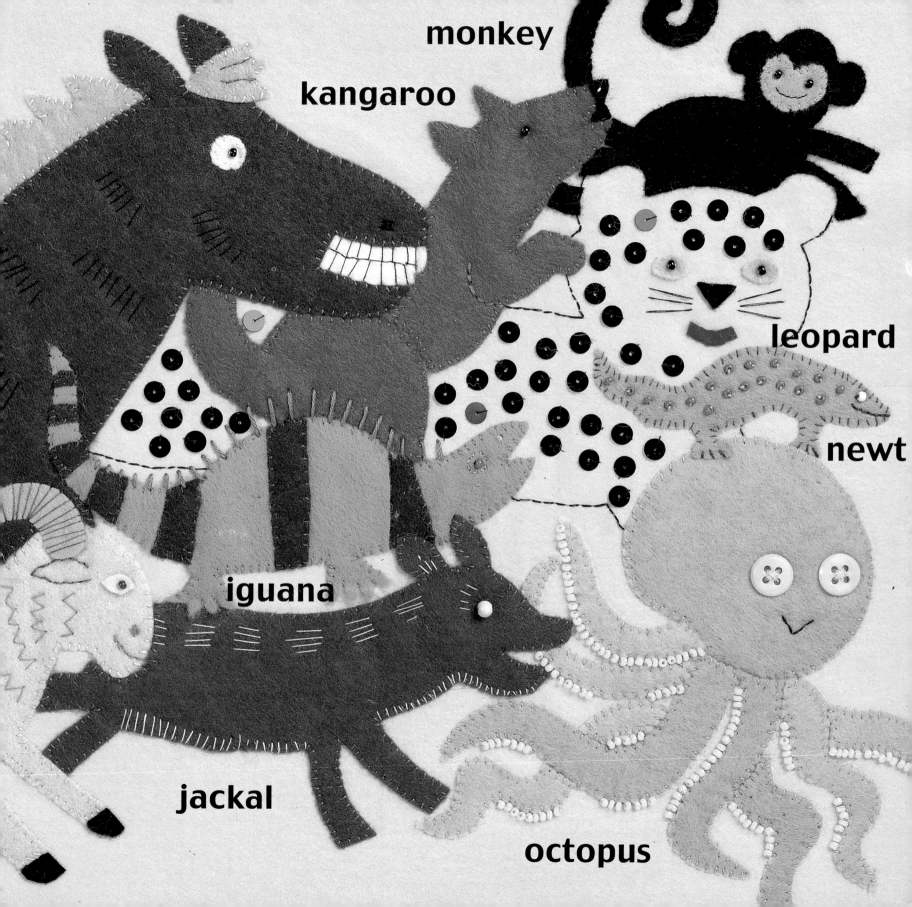

umbrella bird

vulture

wolf

tiger

xoona mo

snake

zebra

quail

rabbit

porcupine

yak

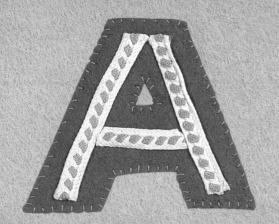

BAREFOOT BOOKS publishes high-quality picture books for children of all ages and specializes in the work of artists and writers from many cultures. If you have enjoyed this book and would like to receive a copy of our current catalog, please contact our New York office —
tel: 718 260 8946   fax: 1 888 346 9138 (toll free)
e-mail: ussales@barefoot-books.com   website: www.barefoot-books.com

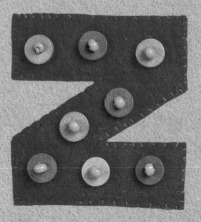

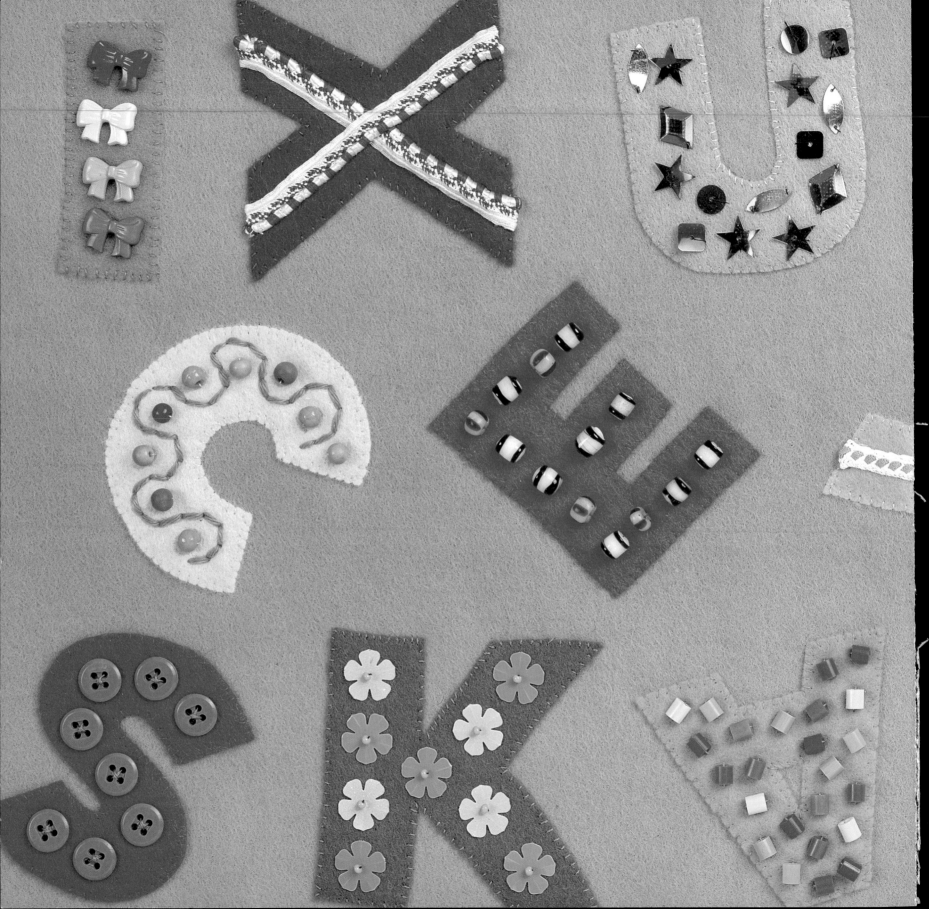